THE
FOX AND THE
GHOST
KING

MICHAEL MORPURGO OBE is one of Britain's best-loved writers for children. He has written over 100 books and won many prizes, including the Smarties Prize, the Blue Peter Book Award and the Whitbread Award. His recent bestselling novels include *An Eagle in the Snow*, *Listen to the Moon* and *A Medal for Leroy*.

Michael's stories have been adapted numerous times for stage and screen, and he was Children's Laureate from 2003 to 2005, a role which took him all over the country to inspire children with the joy of reading stories.

Also by Michael Morpurgo

michael morpurgo

THE FOX AND THE GHOST KING

ILLUSTRATED BY MICHAEL FOREMAN

HarperCollins *Children's Books*

First published in hardback in Great Britain by HarperCollins *Children's Books* in 2016
This edition published in Great Britain by HarperCollins *Children's Books* in 2017
HarperCollins *Children's Books* is a division of HarperCollins*Publishers* Ltd,
1 London Bridge Street, London, SE1 9GF

The HarperCollins website address is:
www.harpercollins.co.uk

5

Text copyright © Michael Morpurgo 2016
Illustrations copyright © Michael Foreman 2016
Photographs in end material © Shutterstock.com

ISBN: 978-00-0-821580-4

Michael Morpurgo and Michael Foreman assert the moral right
to be identified as the author and illustrator of the work.

Printed and bound in England by CPI Group (UK) Ltd, Croydon CR0 4YY

MIX
Paper from
responsible sources
FSC™ C007454

FSC™ is a non-profit international organisation established to promote
the responsible management of the world's forests. Products carrying the
FSC label are independently certified to assure consumers that they come
from forests that are managed to meet the social, economic and
ecological needs of present and future generations,
and other controlled sources.

Find out more about HarperCollins and the environment at
www.harpercollins.co.uk/green

For Jonathan, charioteer supreme,
and his family.

Remembering our journey from
Kettering to Exeter.

~ Contents ~

THE *LEICESTER ECHO*

LEICESTER'S LUCKY FOXES

This season a foxy football fan seems to have become a regular at the Leicester City ground. There are reports that several fans have seen him leaving the ground after evening matches. And there have even been possible sightings of him during daylight matches too. Sometimes he comes alone, but more often these days he brings a cub along with him. And whenever the cub comes along Leicester seem to win. Fans are always delighted, of course, to spot them, because with every game Leicester City play they seem to be getting better, scoring more goals. The more the foxes are seen together at the ground, the more the players and fans believe they can win. They have become Leicester's Lucky Foxes.

~ Prologue ~

On moonlit nights we still often get together. We usually meet on the football pitch, after a match, because it's quiet, no one about. That's how foxes and ghosts like it. It's only when all of us are together again that I

can really believe it happened, that we really did make not just one but two impossible dreams come true.

I have to pinch myself – sometimes even then – to believe it happened. But I was there. I saw it all with my own eyes, heard it with my own ears, smelt it with my own nose.

Honest. Cub's honour. Dib, dib, dib!

1

~ Over the Moon ~

Imagine a family of foxes – Mum, Dad and the four of us little cubs – living in our den under a garden shed in Leicester. That's us. I am the oldest, and I am the boss cub too, the friskiest, the peskiest, the pushiest. Dad likes

that because it reminds him of himself, he says. And that's why, if I pester him enough, he takes me out with him, now that I'm a little older, when he goes on his hunting expeditions at night. Mum never does, because she says she hunts better without me there to worry about. And it's true; she always brings back a fat rabbit or a rat or a mole or a vole every time she goes out. Mum's milk is so good and tasty and there's always enough for all of us. But she does snap at me when I push my sisters off to get the best place to feed.

Dad never snaps at me. He's a good hunter too, but he prefers dustbins, he says, because they don't run away, and they're full of tasty surprises. He hunts pizza crusts, and chips – my favourite, because I love tomato sauce – and chewy Chinese

spare ribs, bits of burgers and buns –
all great stuff. He's the best dustbin
hunter in the world, my dad, and he's
the top fox around, top dad too.

He's not afraid of anyone, or anything, not ghosts, not kings, not even ghost kings – as you will see.

But the most important thing you have to know about our family is that all of us are football crazy: Leicester City fans, Foxes fans. The Foxes are our team, win or lose – mostly lose – the best team in the world.

Every fox in the whole town, in the whole country just about, is a

Foxes football fan. We foxes are brought up Foxes fans.

All his life Dad has been going to the home games; Mum too, when she can, when she's not having cubs. Down in our smelly old den – we like it smelly – all the talk is of football, or food. We talk a lot about food, it's true: pizzas, worms, frogs, mice, chips – especially chips. A varied diet we have.

So you can imagine how excited I

was when Dad asked me for the first time, one winter's night, to come with him to the football. I felt at long last I was becoming a proper grown-up fox. All I wanted now was my silly droopy, drippy little tail to grow into a proper brush, like Dad's. Once you've got a proper brush for a tail, then you're a proper fox, but I was off to my first football match and that was good enough for me.

Over the moon, I was.

I loved it that first time I went, and every time afterwards, the lights, the roar of the crowd, the smell of hot dogs, the music, the singing, the chanting. The losing wasn't so great. Dad always said then that the referee was rubbish, that he had favoured the other side.

He hated Chelsea especially, so did I, especially their manager. He was such a cocky-looking fellow.

I went with him after that whenever I could, whenever Mum would let me go. She worried about me, but mums do that. It's their job.

The night this story began was the night we lost to Chelsea, again, a night we'll never forget, but not because of losing to Chelsea.

No, not because of that at all.

Because of the ghost we met afterwards.

2

~ Weird or What? ~

We were not happy foxes on our way home. Dad was going on about how Mourinho, the Chelsea manager, would be crowing like a cockerel, and how foxes knew how to deal with cockerels.

"Give him a good neck-shaking I would, then gobble him up," he was saying. But we did pick up titbits of this and that from the pavement, leftovers: hotdogs and beef burgers, and fish and chips. You would not believe the stuff people throw away, but I'm glad they do. After that we knocked over a couple of dustbins and found some dribbly ice cream and some mouldy old cheese, which was delicious. We were trying to make ourselves feel a bit better, and we did too. So the Foxes had lost again. So what was new about that?

"Always look on the bright side of life, eh, son? Not the end of the world," he said as we padded along homewards, down the lamp-lit city street. "The Foxes are still the best team in the world, son, right?"

"Right," I told him. We stopped to

do a high-five together, then chased our tails round and round three times – three times would bring us luck the next time, Dad said. I didn't believe him, of course. We did the same every time we lost, and we still lost the next time. I knew really that he made me do it to cheer me up, and to cheer himself up too.

A little while later, and happier now, we were on our usual way home,

trotting through the empty car park, half of which was still being dug up, for some reason or other. We always stopped here, because the earth was always freshly turned, just right for worm hunting.

We leapt the fence – well, Dad did; I crawled underneath – then jumped down into a shallow trench and, noses to the ground, began sniffing out worms, and listening for them too.

We can hear worms wriggling, you know; it's what we've got these pointy ears for.

I was good at worm-catching – watched Dad doing it and just did what he did – loved it too, the snuffling them out, the watching, the waiting, then, best of all, the leaping and pouncing.

I was happily chomping away on the nice fat wriggly worm I had just caught, which was trying to curl itself round my nose, when I thought I heard a strange voice. It seemed close by and yet far away at the same time. And somehow it was coming from below me too.

Weird or what? I thought.

Dad had heard it as well. His ears were pricked, turning, turning, this way and that, and that way and this.

Then the voice spoke again, definitely a man's voice, and it really was coming from somewhere deep down below the ground.

"I know a fox when I smell one,"
it said. "You all wear your smell
about you like a coat of rank
and rotten onions."

I could feel the hair standing up in fear all along the back of my neck. But Dad wasn't frightened, so after a moment or two I wasn't either. Like me, he was looking for the voice, trying to smell and hear exactly where it might be coming from. So I did the same.

Dad spoke then, in his growliest angriest voice: "I don't know who you are, but how we smell is our business. So, whoever and wherever you are, you have no business making rude remarks to strangers you have never even met, and who mean you no harm and have never hurt you. I have my son with me. I have brought him up never to be rude. So mind your manners, stranger, whoever you are. And there's something else I want to tell you: all onions are delicious, rotten or not. Especially old pizza onions in tomato sauce, however rotten they are."

"I do not wish to discuss onions, Mister Fox," the voice came again. "I have much more important things on my mind."

"Such as?" Dad asked.

"Such as getting out of here," came the reply. "I have been stuck down here for hundreds of years, and I need to get out. You must help me. It is my command, and I am used to people doing what I say when I say it."

He was sounding rather hoity-toity, and I could see Dad did not like being told what to do by this voice one bit.

Dad told him in no uncertain terms, but politely, what he thought of his command. "So don't you come all lah-di-dah and lordly with me. I don't know who you think you are, but if you want our assistance, then you are going to have to explain yourself. How can we possibly help you get out of where you are if we don't even know where that is? And, by the way, we don't know who you are either. You're just a strange, rather snooty, disembodied voice to us at the moment. Where are you? Who are you, for goodness' sake?"

"The king," said the voice, more haughtily even than before. "You are speaking to the King of England, Mister Fox."

3

~ Rotten Onions and High-fives ~

Dad laughed at that. "Yeah, yeah, yeah, course you are! The King of England! So you're one of those, then. Too much to drink, eh? A bit bonkers, off your rocker. I've met lots of your sort before, out in the city at night,

wandering the streets. But I've never met anyone before that I can't see. Never even talked to anyone I can't see. Now, my little son and I have to get home. It's getting late. Goodnight, Your Kingship."

"No, don't go," came the voice again, more polite now, pleading almost. "Please don't go. I would show myself to you if I could. But that's my problem – I can't get out of here. Listen, Mister Fox and Master Fox, all I'm asking is for you to do me a small favour. I want you to show those idiot archaeologists, who are doing all the digging, where I am."

"Arky-what-a-gists?" I asked. "What are they, Dad? What do they do?"

"They do digging, son," Dad told me, "for old stuff, old things."

"Old worms, you mean?" I said.

"Older, son. Bigger. Old buildings, old bits and pieces, anything. They even dig up old people sometimes."

"And sometimes even an old king," came the voice again. "I am not bonkers, not off my rocker, Mister Fox, I promise you. I am just an old king who has been lying down here for hundreds and hundreds of years, and I want to get out. And I won't ever get out if those stupid archaeologists don't find me. Which is why I really need you to lead them to me. They've been digging for me, searching for me for

months and months now, but never in the right place. They keep missing me, just can't seem to find where I am. I've been calling them and calling them, just like I called you, but I don't think they can hear me. Foxes hear better, don't they? You must do. You heard me after all."

"That's because foxes do everything better, don't we, son?" said Dad.

"Right on, Dad," I replied. And

we did our high-fives again.

"And foxes dig well too – am I right?" came the voice.

"We only dig the best tunnels and deepest dens in all the world," Dad told him proudly. "They may smell of rotten onions, but we like home to smell like that, right, son?" We high-fived again.

"Listen, Mister Fox," the voice said, in quite a different tone altogether now.

"I'm really sorry I ever said that, about you smelling like rotten onions. Dastardly thing to say. Pardon me, please. I should be so grateful if you could please dig me one of your best tunnels in the world, towards where I am. I'll just keep talking and you keep digging. It won't take long. You'll find me sooner or later. You can't miss me. I'm not going anywhere, not until you find me anyway."

I could see Dad was thinking long and hard. "Now, let me get this right, Your Kingship," he began. "You want us, me and my little cub here – who by rights should be back home and fast asleep by now down in our smelly den – you want us to get digging and keep digging till we find you. I mean that could take all night, couldn't it? Have you any idea of the trouble I'll be in with the

wife if I stay out all night, if I don't get our little son home till morning? Trouble and strife, Your Kingship, that's what I'll be in for, trouble and strife."

Dad was shaking his head and tutting away. Quite an actor my dad can be.

"But let's just say we oblige you, Your Kingship," he went on, "and we do what you ask, what do we get

in return? I mean, just how grateful would you be, if you see what I'm saying?"

"So foxes are as cunning as they say," came the reply.

"Oh yes indeed, Your Kingship," Dad said. "King or fox, you have to be cunning to survive in this life, as cunning as a fox."

"I cannot argue with you there, Mister Fox. Very well, tell me what it is you most wish for in all the world," said the voice, "and I shall grant it."

"With what power?" asked Dad.

"You can't even tell the archaeologists where you are."

"Only because I have never had a king's burial," said the voice. "Release me, and I can do anything. Just tell me your greatest wish."

4

~ The Promise of a King ~

"That's simple," Dad said, "but it's also quite impossible. We all have an impossible dream. We want our team, Leicester City, to win the next match, don't we, son? And—"

"Easy, it's a deal," the voice

interrupted. "Get me out of here and I'll make sure you win the next match."

"No, no, I hadn't finished, Your Kingship," Dad went on. "We don't just want to win the next match, but the one after, and the next after that, and the next, and go on winning. We want to beat Spurs and Man United, and Man City and Liverpool – wipe the floor with them all, especially Chelsea.

Us, the Foxes, Leicester City, we want
to be top of the Premier League, top of
the world. Me and my little cub here,
and my family and my kind, we have
supported the Foxes for ever. But we
never win a thing. Last season we were
almost bottom of the league, nearly
went down. Do you know, the betting
against us winning the league this
season is five thousand to one? You
help us win the league, Your Kingship,

71

help us achieve the impossible dream, and we'll dig for you, tunnel our way to you, and help get you out of there. That's the deal. Take it or leave it."

"You strike a hard bargain, Mister Fox. Very well. I agree. You have my word. You get me out of here, and I will guarantee your team wins the league this season. And that's a promise."

"Promises, promises," said Dad. "There's always a problem with promises: they are so easy to make, and so easy to break. How, pray, Your Kingship, will you do it? How do we know you can do it, and how can we be sure you will?"

"I do not break my promises. You are speaking to the rightful king of all England, Mister Fox," he said, sounding haughtier again. "What I say

should happen in this land, happens.
I am king, do you hear me? I rule
here! And when I am laid to rest as
befits a king I will be able to do stuff,
make stuff happen, impossible stuff –
'such stuff as dreams are made on . . .'
Oh rats! There I go. You hear that? I
can't seem to help myself. I'm always
quoting that villainous scribbler Will
Shakespeare, that 'rogue and peasant
slave'. Rats! You see? His words again!

They haunt me. He haunts me. He's inside my head: his voice, his words, his poems, his plays. That infernal dramatist haunts my life and my death to this very day."

The voice was becoming more agitated and angry, and louder now, with every word he spoke.

I crept under Dad's brush and hid myself away. But I could not stop myself from trembling.

"Alack, alack," the voice went on, the pitch rising, "but for a horse a kingdom was lost, my kingdom. 'A horse, a horse! My kingdom for a horse!' There I go again! Losing my horse, losing my throne, losing my life on Bosworth Field that day, was bad enough, painful enough too, I can tell you. But worse, so much worse – Will Shakespeare took my reputation. 'Reputation, reputation! Oh, reputation,

I have lost my reputation!' By his play of Richard III, that vile villain made a villain of me, a traitor, a murderer. I may not have been the best of kings, not whiter than white maybe, but not blacker than black either. And who do they celebrate now all over the world? Me? A crowned King of England? No, that wretched man, that ruinous rhymster, that dastardly dramatist, that William Shakespeare.

"And as for me? I end up buried in a car park in Leicester, not in my rightful place, not honoured in a tomb in a cathedral like other kings and queens. But if they find me, these archaeologists, I will be famous again, a king again, and honoured. The people, history, may even begin to remember me as I was, not as that which Shakespeare made me to be. Just get me out of this horrible car park, I beg you, my foxy friends, and I will ensure the Foxes of Leicester City win the league. You have my promise, the promise of a king."

Well, Dad liked digging anyway. So did I. What had we got to lose? You get worms if you dig, great fat wriggly ones if you're lucky.

And if the king kept his promise we would be getting a lot more

than worms for the Foxes, for

Leicester City.

So we dug.

5

~ Digging and Dreaming ~

We dug down and down, deep under the car park, then along and along, Dad digging – Dad doing most of the digging, if I'm honest – with me scooping out the earth behind us.

We dug, and scooped, and dug

and scooped, and the king's voice talked us in towards him all the time, mostly about that wretched horse of his that ran off just before they killed him at Bosworth Field, and how you should never trust a war horse. They're not brave at all, he said, just big, and stupid. And of course he went on and on about how much he loathed and detested and despised William Shakespeare.

Dad didn't like to upset him, but he told me quietly, as he was digging, that he had once watched one of those Shakespeare plays, an open-air production in the park, and it wasn't bad at all, he said. *A Midsummer Night's Dream* he thought it was called. He wasn't sure he quite understood the story, but there were a lot of laughs, and a donkey called Bottom, he remembered, and a funny

little fellow, a wild creature of the

woods, called Puck.

"A bit like a fox, he was," said

Dad, digging away. "A bit like me, bit like you. He kept getting himself into all sorts of trouble, but somehow managed to get himself out of it again. Like I said, like us!"

It was a tiring night and a long night. But we kept ourselves digging by telling each other what the scores were going to be in every match the Foxes would be playing in their winning season ahead.

We lived every game as we imagined it: who scored the goals – so Vardy mostly, of course – who made the tackles, the crosses, the perfect passes, who took the penalties.

Spurs 0 – Leicester City 4!

Manchester United 1 – Leicester City 3!

Southampton 1 – Leicester City 6!

Chelsea 0 – Leicester City 10!

The more we won, "in our mind's eye" – that's Shakespeare again (he gets everywhere that man, like the king said) – the more goals we scored, the harder we dug. We ate a few worms as we went along, of course, to keep ourselves going.

By dawn we were that close to the king's voice we thought we could almost smell him.

"They'll find you easily enough now, Your Kingship," said Dad. "And we've got to get home before the

city wakes up."

The king thanked us quite politely.

But Dad was not fooled by politeness. "When they find you, Your Kingship, you just keep your side of the bargain. All right?" he told him, politely but very firmly.

"I will," said the king. "Don't you worry, Mister Fox, Master Fox, I will. I am a king of my word."

So we padded back along the streets, visiting a dustbin here and there on the way, and came back to our lovely warm smelly den under the garden shed, where we told Mum and all my little sisters everything that had happened.

And Mum was cross with us. We had stayed out so late, and she'd been worried sick, she said. Also she thought that digging all night, just because some strange voice from under the ground asked us to, and for a ridiculous promise that could never come true, was a waste of time and plain silly. And my sisters were cross because Dad had not brought home any pizza or chips for them, and they were jealous I had had such an exciting time.

They wanted to go to the football as much as me, and it wasn't fair, they

said. They do go on sometimes, my sisters. But I love them all the same.

And when I slept that night, I dreamed the impossible dream: the Foxes had won the league, and Vardy was holding the cup aloft and everyone in Leicester, and every fox in the whole country was over the moon, on Cloud Nine – well, you know what I mean.

And do you know? They

discovered the grave of Richard III in the car park – followed our tunnel and found it – the very next day. They even said some fox had led them right to it. It was two foxes actually.

And after a bit of historical. and political kerfuffle and argy-bargy, they buried him, with all the pomp and honour and dignity he had so longed for, in Leicester Cathedral. And do you know something else?

"...they buried him,
with all the pomp and
honour and dignity he had
so longed for..."

William Shakespeare was wrong about that king, in part at least. King Richard III of England was not as bad as all that, as Shakespeare had made him out to be.

He was a king of his word. He kept his promise.

6

Is This a Pizza
~ I See Before Me? ~

How he kept his promise we did not know, and we did not care.

Right from the start of the season Leicester City, our wonderful Foxes, just started winning. The very first match we beat Sunderland 4–2. Easy peasy.

We came back from two goals down to beat Aston Villa 3–2, scoring three goals in the last twenty minutes. Easy peasy.

Soon we were up to fifth place in the league. We were there at every home match, not just Dad and me, but the whole family now. Dad and me came for the football, of course, for the Foxes, but Mum and my sisters came for the easy pickings after the match:

the hotdog rolls soaked in tomato sauce, the left-behind pizza slices.

But we were worried. We were letting in too many goals, not beating everyone the way we needed to if we were going to win the league, like he had promised us.

But the Ghost King was not bothered, not one bit. "Don't you worry, my friends," he told us. "I had a word with the manager, that Ranieri

fellow – I told him in a dream. I said, 'Use bribery; it's the only way.' Kings know these things."

Next thing we heard that Ranieri had promised the players that whenever they kept a clean sheet, no goals scored against them, then he would give them all a treat and take them out for a pizza.

It worked a treat too! The Foxes chased and chased, tackled and tackled; the goalkeeper saved goal after goal.

We were there at the Crystal Palace match, the whole family of us foxes, cheering them on, and we were there too down the alleyway at the back of the pizzeria after we had beaten them 1–0, not letting in a single goal, and the players were inside scoffing their pizzas.

*

"*It worked a treat too!*"

We waited until they'd finished, then knocked over the dustbins outside and scoffed the leftovers – theirs and everyone else's. We were chomping away on our heroes' pizzas! Best pizzas I ever had!

That was the match when we all began to believe the impossible dream might happen – my little sisters too, Mum as well. They were loving the football now as much as the pizzas.

Is This a Pizza I See Before Me?

After that Crystal Palace match, we just went on winning, and Ranieri kept taking the team out for pizzas, because so few sides could ever score against us.

7

~ All's Well That Ends Well ~

We were there on another moonlit night, a year or so later, out on the Leicester City football pitch the day they won the Premier League. The whole city was going bananas. Every fox all over the land, in towns and

villages, in city parks and countryside, was barking at the moon.

But the football stadium in Leicester was quiet, not a soul about. Leicester weren't even playing that day: it was Chelsea drawing against Tottenham that gave our beloved Foxes the points to win the Premier League, and that only made Dad and me happier.

All of us were there on the empty pitch in the empty stadium, the whole family, my sisters too, and the Ghost King, our friend who had made it all happen, just as he had promised it would.

"So are you happy foxes tonight?" the Ghost King asked. He was a bit see-through this ghost, but ghosts are. You get used to it. He wasn't a bit frightening – weird, but not frightening.

"Tonight every fox all over the

country is happy, thanks to you, Your Kingship," said Dad. "But how on earth did you manage to do it?"

"I told you, a king can do stuff, and a ghost king can do even more, once he's free."

"'Such stuff as dreams are made on'?" said Dad.

"That Shakespeare fellow, he's inside your head now, isn't he?"

"Which reminds me," Dad said. "They're putting on the play of *A Midsummer Night's Dream* again, in the park next Saturday. We're all going. Do you want to come along?"

So we went, all of us together.

A lovely summer's evening. Dad was right. That Puck really is a wild spirit of the woods, a bit like him, a bit like me, a bit like all of us foxes – just foxy! And Dad was right too about William Shakespeare – he makes wonderful plays.

Even the Ghost King thought so, reluctantly maybe, but he couldn't hide it. As we walked away, he whispered just loud enough for all of us to hear:

"'All's well that ends well.'"

"Right on, Your Kingship," I said.

And we all did high-fives together,

the Ghost King too.

THE *LEICESTER ECHO*

HOW THE IMPOSSIBLE DREAM
CAME TRUE.

Was it the manager? Was it the team? Was it the fans? How on earth did the Foxes, 5,000 to 1 outsiders at the beginning of the season, manage to make our impossible dream come true and become Premier League champions? Some say it was the work of the grateful spirit of Richard III, rescued from his grave in the car park a year ago, and now buried in our cathedral. There have been numerous reported sightings of a ghostly figure wafting through the city late at night. Some say he looks a bit like Laurence Olivier, others that he more resembles Benedict Cumberbatch, both of whom have played him onscreen.

But most now believe our miraculous success is down to the presence amongst the fans, at every home match this season, of a family of foxes, six of them, Leicester's lucky foxes! Sightings of them have been more reliable than the stories of our wandering ghost king. Foxes smell something awful. I have smelt them myself, often at the King Power Stadium, so they were definitely there! Thank you, foxes! Thank you.

A Note on Leicester City F.C.

By Michael Foreman

In 1884, a group of old boys from Wyggeston School in Leicester formed a football team and played on a field near Fosse Road. They called the team *Leicester Fosse* and eventually joined the Football Association in 1890.

In 1908, they gained promotion to the First Division (the highest level of

The Leicester Fosse team of 1892

English football at the time) but were relegated the very next season.

So began a century-long see-saw pattern of promotion and numerous relegations. Their highest position during all this time was second in Division 1 in 1929.

In 2002, the club hit their lowest point by going into administration with debts of £30m, to be followed in 2008 by relegation to the third tier of English football – their lowest ever position.

Then . . . in August 2012, King Richard III was found under a Leicester car park, and a right royal turnaround in the Foxes' fortunes began, with their long-awaited return to the top flight, the Premier League, in 2014.

After narrowly avoiding relegation again at the end of the season, they started the 2015/16 season as favourites to be relegated. Bookmakers assessed their chances of winning the Premier League at 5,000 to 1.

However, as the whole world now knows, after an amazing season the Foxes were CROWNED CHAMPIONS!

A Note on Richard III

By Michael Morpurgo

History in the United Kingdom was never more horrible than during the long civil war in the fifteenth century, which came to be called the Wars of the Roses – the struggle for the crown between the White Rose of the Yorkists and the Red Rose of the Lancastrians.

This war raged on for decades,

and was essentially a family squabble about which line had the most rights to the throne, this son or that cousin, the Yorkist side of the line or the Lancastrian.

It became a brutal and cruel conflict and drew in the whole country. Sometimes the Lancastrian followers of Red Rose seemed to be winning, and then the White Rose of the Yorkists had their man on the throne.

The kings – Henry, Edward and Richard – may have different names

The Wars of the Roses

and numbers, may have been White Rose or Red Rose, but all were soon deposed or killed.

Betrayal was rampant; people and families changed sides depending on which way the wind of opportunity seemed to be blowing. Battles raged as the power ebbed one way, then the other. Opponents were imprisoned, banished, murdered or executed, in an effort to establish supremacy. It was an era of terrible tyranny and great suffering.

By means just as devious and ruthless and murderous as his predecessors – but not a lot worse – Richard III of the House of York, and therefore champion of the White Rose Yorkist family faction, manoeuvred

Richard III

and murdered his way to the throne in

the year 1483 at the age of thirty.

Shakespeare and others painted

him as the cruellest of kings, largely because of the murder of the two young princes in the tower, his rivals to the throne. Whether Richard ordered this "disappearance" or simply allowed it to happen, we cannot be sure. We cannot even be certain that the boys died. But they *did* disappear and they had as rightful a claim to the throne as did Richard III. Who knows how guilty he was?

It was Shakespeare who made up our mind about him for us by writing his play *Richard III*, in which the king became the most villainous and reviled in our history. Two great actors, Laurence Olivier first, and in recent times, Benedict Cumberbatch, in their dark portrayals of Richard III, have confirmed him as the personification of cunning, ambition and evil.

Richard's short reign came to an end at the Battle of Bosworth Field in 1485, where he met the army of Henry Tudor, the Red Rose and Lancastrian claimant to the throne. The story goes that in the battle Richard fell off his horse, could not find it again, and was surrounded by Henry's soldiers. They cut him down and killed him. His body was later taken to a monastery in Leicester where it was buried hurriedly and without ceremony in an unmarked grave.

Hundreds of years later, his body was discovered, under what had since become a car park. The rest, as they say, is history. He was buried finally in Leicester Cathedral; and, shortly after,